1, 2, 3, Music!

Sylvie Auzary-Luton

ORCHARD BOOKS • NEW YORK

nnie was hanging out the laundry and listening to her Walkman®.

"Aren't you a darling," said Grandma as she came
home from shopping. "Go ahead and play now,
honey. I'll finish up." But Annie couldn't hear her.

She twirled around . . . and over went the basket of laundry!

Baby Tom started crying, and Grandma got mad. "Annie! I like music, too, but that thing you wear on your ears is impossible. You never hear anything anymore."

"There, there," said Grandpa. "Baby Tom was just surprised, that's all. Why don't you go play with your cousins, Annie."

Annie picked up a stick and broke it in half.

Poor Annie. She had wrecked her cousins' sand castle.

"I didn't mean to."

But as she listened to her music, Annie cheered up. Her feet started tapping, her fingers started snapping, and her head started rocking from side to side.

Then Annie jumped up.

She twisted and twirled and turned.

Her grandmother came running. "Goodness gracious!" she exclaimed. "That Walkman® is horrible. You can't be by yourself all the time jumping around with that thing over your ears. Now give it to me, and go play with your cousins."

"Okay, Grandma," said Annie.

But Annie knew her cousins were still upset with her. She sat by herself—and heard music!

It was a street band. How wonderful! thought Annie, and she began to clap along.

Then she heard her cousins laughing.

"There's nothing wrong with loving music!" Annie cried. "You just don't understand! You don't know how to listen!"

Annie ran upstairs in tears.

She threw herself on an old trunk. "I'm going to run away! I'll be a musician in an orchestra." She hit the trunk with her fist . . . and the trunk answered!

BONG

Clink

"What was that?" Annie wondered. She opened the trunk and found some old photos. "Oh! It's Grandpa! He was the trumpet player in an orchestra? Wow!"

She dug deeper in the trunk. . . .

Wow! A trumpet! A drum!
A xylophone! A banjo!
A concertina! A tambourine and
bells! Hooray! Grandpa must have
saved these from when he was
in a band!

She tried them all, one after the other,

the trumpet,   the drum,   the xylophone,

the banjo,   the concertina,   the tambourine and the bells.

So she did.

She blew and banged
and marched.

But the instruments were too heavy. Annie fell over backward with a loud crash.

BOOM

Her cousins came running.

They each grabbed an instrument and started to play. Annie was beaming.

They made such a racket that their grandfather came up to the attic to see what was going on. When he saw them, he laughed. "I should have known you'd find my instruments."

"Grandpa, will you teach us?" begged Annie.

"Oh yes! Please, Grandpa," cried her cousins.

Grandpa picked up the trumpet. "I'll help you get started, but, you know, Annie is a natural. She has a great sense of rhythm, and you could learn a lot from her." Annie's cousins looked at her and smiled. Annie was thrilled.

Tap! Tap! Tap! Follow the beat of the trumpet. One, two, three, music!

Grandma came running. "Ouch, my ears!" she shouted. "The neighbors just called to say you are making too much noise."

Grandpa turned around. "Tell them this is a big day. There's a new band in the neighborhood, and we need to practice. Invite them all over on Saturday for the first performance of Annie's Band."

Grandma smiled. "How exciting! I'm going to get out my dancing shoes! Thanks, Annie."